Something is Something

Steve Gallegos

Moon Bear Press

Something is Something

Steve Gallegos.

Printing History
First Edition
1st printing: August 2014

Cover:
Artist: Barbara Reiter (Giraffe)
reiter-frabertsham@t-online.de
Composition: Mary Diggin

ISBN 978-0-944164-28-0 (Print)
ISBN 978-0-944164-29-7 (Kindle)

Moon Bear Press
PO Box 468
Velarde NM 87582
orders@moonbearpress.com
www.moonbearpress.com

Contents

The Visit

The visit was a surprise to his parents. David knocked at the door of the house where he had grown up, his mother, looking older but happy, came to the door, stared at him for a few seconds and then exploded in tears of joy.

"David! David!" she exclaimed, almost speechless. We didn't know what to think after you had been summoned to the Governor's program. How long ago was that? Four years? Five years ago? We tried to find out where the program was but the government seemed to want to keep it secret, so we thought it must be something very special. Come in! Come in!"

David entered the house. It was much smaller now,

smaller than he remembered it being. Father was not at home but a young child came running in.

"Mommy, Mommy. Who is it?" she asked. She looked at David with giant eyes and then said, "Is this David?"

"Yes, Cornelia, this is your big brother David that we told you about. He's been off at a special school where he went shortly before you were born. Look how big he is. My, how you have grown, David."

David was speechless. Then he suddenly remembered something secretive taking place between his parents and learning that they were expecting another baby. But he had not thought about it since leaving with Grandfather. Cornelia must have been born not long after he had left.

He suddenly remembered that a little brother had been born when he was still quite young, and he had sadly died only a month after he was born. Great sadness had loomed in the home after his death, and no one wanted to talk about it, or to explain to David just what Death was, or what had really happened to Jeremy. It had left him feeling blank and unsure of himself, like there were things he was not supposed to know nor to ask about. It had caused him to go quiet and to turn inward.

Now he understood why Mother and Father had been so quiet when she was pregnant with Cornelia. They were afraid that she might also die and so they were wary of saying too much, and they didn't want David to begin asking questions about Death again. Their pain from Jeremy's death was still very tangible.

Cornelia had great big eyes that looked inquisitively at David. He was a mystery to her, and there was also something very magical about the energy between these two siblings. David sat down on the couch and Cornelia immediately sat next to him and said, "Tell me about all your adventures in the big world!"

Where to Begin

David didn't know where to begin. As he sat on the couch with the new sister he had just met he thought of Grandfather, and of Bearman, and of the village where he had come to feel so at home, more at home than he had ever felt here in the house where he had been born and where he had spent his childhood years. This house felt so confining now, so tiny, so shielded from the natural world that he had grown to love and to feel a deep kinship with. He recognized how deeply the natural wildness of the mountains and the sea had become a part of him. That entire wild area had become his home now and this tiny house where he sat on the couch with Cornelia with his mother looking on in anticipation felt more like a prison where aliveness was very limited and restricted. How could he even begin to tell Cornelia or mother about what he now knew. He realized they would not understand, and that Mother would feel it a criticism of all that she had done.

David recalled the talks he and Grandfather had had.

He recalled Grandfather telling him that some people built their own cages in order to feel safe without realizing that they were imprisoning themselves.

"They do that not only with these limiting enclosures that they call houses, but they do that also with their thinking," Grandfather had said. "They build enclosures of thought that they feel safe in and are threatened by the thinking of others. They can only recognize whether other people's thinking fits the same pattern as their own and if it doesn't they start talking faster and louder in order to fight off the thoughts that they feel as threats. Such people confuse their thinking with the actuality of who they are. They don't recognize that thinking is merely a postulation of possibilities and that as they experience their aliveness these possibilities change. Thinking is supposed to be alive and dancing, but many people have frozen it into blocks of ice."

David could feel Mother's anticipation and expectation as if it were an electric energy in the room, whereas Cornelia's energy was open and curious, the energy of exploration and excitement. And David realized that whatever he said would be heard differently by these two loving beings so he proceeded slowly and he spoke so that Mother's fears would not be disturbed but he was also focussed on Cornelia's excited receptivity. David understood immediately that in spite of their close relationship Cornelia and Mother lived in two very different worlds.

"The school that I attended," he began, looking at Mother, "was an exciting school where learning was really alive. I had to learn not just from books but from some very powerful adventures that were a part of the curriculum. My teachers were very learned and experienced, with ways of teaching that were beyond anything I had experienced in the small school here."

Then he looked at Cornelia, smiled, and continued. "It was a school where I learned not only with my mind but with everything that I am. It was a school that used the natural world as its setting and its laboratories, and we learned from everything that happens. Oh, it is so difficult to describe because it is so unlike our usual schools."

"Well, it sounds very different," Mother said. "And I can see that you've grown bigger and much stronger than you were when you left. But I don't understand why we couldn't visit you there. We tried to find out by writing to the Governor's office where it was but we received the strangest replies, and it felt like they just wanted to keep the whole thing secret."

"Yes," said David. "It's a new experimental school and they wanted to validate its methods before it was made generally known to the public. That's why the students were so secretly and specifically selected. I was very lucky to have been chosen."

"I want to go there!" Cornelia replied excitedly.

Cornelia

What David had told his mother and Cornelia was not really a lie. Grandfather had told David that it was wrong to lie and in fact David had already learned that long ago. But Grandfather had also taught David that you had to use words that could be understood by the person you were talking to. David knew that if he were to describe his meeting with the Bear in the mountains that Mother would have been shocked and terrified, and would never have understood what an important learning this had been for David. In fact, she would have stopped listening to David and would have gotten embroiled in everything that she feared. That would have been the end of any communication with her. David would have loved to have her understand the beauty of everything he had experienced in the village but he knew he had to tell her very gradually so that she would not get lost in her own unresolved emotions. David could see the cage of words and feelings that she lived in and he knew it was not easy to help a person get beyond these.

Especially if they were not ready to. And David hoped that some day he would be able to help Mother return to the foundation of her natural aliveness rather than living in the cage of her words and unresolved feelings, just as Grandfather had helped him to do, but he also knew that it would have to happen very gradually.

But Cornelia was a different matter. David could feel the surge of her aliveness, the pull of her curiosity and her strong will to know a bigger world. He knew she was at a place where she was really ready to grow. Mother suddenly said, "I've got to go finish preparing supper, your father will be home soon. Cornelia, why don't you go show David how we have decorated the room he used to live in and made it yours."

"Yes, I'd love to see it. What have you done to it?"

Cornelia was delighted to take David to see her room. And he was surprised at the great change. The few posters he had on the wall were no longer there and the room had been painted pink and soft blue. There were frilly curtains on the windows and the bed was piled high with soft stuffed animals and dolls. David suddenly had an idea of how he could begin to help Cornelia.

"Which is your favorite animal?" he asked her.

"Oh, I love the Giraffe," she answered immediately, picking up the soft giraffe with a long neck and hugging it.

"What is Giraffe's name?"

"Oh, I call her Jessie."

"So Jessie's a girl?"

"A girl Giraffe, silly."

"Does Jessie ever talk to you?"

"Of course! How do you think I know her name?"

David was delighted to hear these answers. "I had an Elephant that used to talk to me when I was younger. But no one could see him and I never told Mom and Dad about him," said David, knowing that he was deliberately telling another human about Elephant for the very first time.

Cornelia stared at David with an unsettling look.

Dad

Dad arrived home and was shocked to see how big David had grown, he was bigger than Dad. Not only that but he was husky, strong, muscular, like an athlete, but an athlete skilled in dance, lithe, quick and yet there was also a stillness in him. Dad was very taken aback. His son was much more mature than he was and he had no experience in how to react to this. Dad was very happy to see David, for even in all his confusion he loved David, but he had no idea how to be with David. He felt he needed to play the role of father yet he felt much smaller and younger than his own son. Dad was confused, but it was really only a part of the confusion he had always felt. It was not really anything new.

By then Mother had prepared supper and they all sat down at the table.

Cornelia couldn't wait to begin talking: "David told me

that when he was a little boy he had a toy elephant that he used to talk to just like I talk to my toy animals and dolls."

Both parents sat in shocked surprise.

Mother said: "David, I don't remember you having a toy elephant."

Cornelia continued in a great rush: "Only it wasn't a real toy elephant but a pretend toy elephant that no one else could see. And he never told anyone else about it."

David was just as shocked as his parents, for he had intended this to be a private communication between himself and Cornelia. He suddenly realized that Cornelia was much more open with her parents than he had been as a child. She seemed to have no protective boundaries around what she said to them. She seemed unafraid of their comments and judgement, and David began to see that the emotional environment he had grown up in was much different from that of Cornelia. He also began to consider that perhaps he wasn't the only one to have changed during these past years while he was at the village. Maybe his parents had also changed?

Father seemed to be getting more and more uncomfortable and said: "Mother, this is a fine dinner that you have prepared for us."

But Cornelia was unstoppable: "I'm so happy to get to finally meet you, David. Mother and Father always told me I had a big brother but I didn't know he was as big and as strong as you. I really want to hear about your adventures. And why didn't you write more? Mother and Father were very proud and happy to get your letters while you were away, but there were so few of them. They would read them to me but you never told us very much about what you were studying and about where the school was so that we could go and visit you."

Stories

David knew that he would have to tell them some stories about the time he had been away. And he knew the stories must be truthful, yet he also understood he would have to speak in a language that his parents understood. He would have to talk in the ideas that they knew, at least at first, perhaps later they would be open to hearing things that were more precise and true to his own experience, and to what he had experienced with Bearman and Grandfather. So he began by translating some of the events into the language that his parents knew about school.

"First of all, it was a very full curriculum," he said. "So there was very little time to write or for personal events. The school was an experiential school, like a natural laboratory, full of individual experiences in the way that nature functions. The professors were highly qualified in their particular fields and were relentless in their supervision of the student's activities and schoolwork. We were active from daybreak until sundown, so that all I could do at night was to sleep deeply. There was really no time to go to the movies or to hang around street corners." He smiled as he said this.

Mother and Father nodded knowingly and with fond approval. They understood that David's time had been well spent in learning and the elegance of his language testified to this.

Father said: "It sounds like a fantastic school, but I don't understand why it has been kept so secret. The Governor's Office was unwilling to tell us anything at all about it. We wrote to them several times inquiring about you and about the school and they seemed to insist on keeping everything secret."

"Yes," said David, "since it is a pilot program they want to study the results thoroughly before it is instituted on a broader scale. It was an honor to have been selected for such a specialized program. It was especially appreciated that you both had allowed me to enter this program given such short notice."

"Yes, well, we trust the governor and the way he runs this state," said Father, with not a little pride in his voice.

Cornelia's Dream

Just as Father finished speaking Cornelia suddenly blurted out: "I just remembered the dream I had last night! It was scary!"

"In the dream Mother was reading me a story and I was all excited because I was getting ready to start school. And I knew I would be learning to read and to write. I love the stories that Mother reads to me every night when I go to bed and I was so happy because I knew I would be learning to read stories myself and also to write stories. While she was reading to me I fell asleep and I was walking to school with Jessie and we were both really happy and excited. On the path to school we had to go through a tunnel that went under the street, and as we were going through it the tunnel got littler and littler until it was very tiny and we could just barely crawl along and it got so tiny that Jessie couldn't go any farther because she was so tall so I had to leave her behind. I started to cry because I didn't want to leave her. Her body didn't fit in the tunnel any more because it was so tight and so she stretched her neck out and I carried her head with me and her neck got skinnier and skinnier and then her head was too big and so she stuck out her tongue and it got longer and I just had her tongue in my hand but then it got too slippery and I suddenly let go of it and it was dark and I was very scared and I started to cry and then I woke up but I was still scared."

Mother said, "Oh, Cornelia, it was just a dream, it wasn't real, you don't need to pay any attention to it. Come, eat your supper."

David knew he had returned home just in time!

The Guest Room

That evening was relatively uncomfortable. The family sat around the TV set watching the evening news until Father announced that he had some work to do and left. Mother seemed unwilling to ask David more about his school, almost as if she really didn't want to know anything more. David was glad he didn't have to translate any more about his life for the past few years, but Cornelia was very intense and kept looking at David as if she needed to learn more about him but she didn't inquire further.

Suddenly Mother announced that she was very tired and that it was also Cornelia's bed time, and that she hoped David would be comfortable sleeping in the guest bedroom.

Alone in the guest bedroom David's mind was racing. He had never slept in this room before and since they seldom had guests the room had been used mainly for storage and for hanging extra clothes in the closet. The bed was stiff and cold and David longed for the lovely soft furs that he had slept under in the longhouse. Everything here felt so sterile and lifeless, even his parents felt like they had each retreated to the very center of their cages and were even afraid to approach their own boundaries and meet the world. David understood that there were elements of their own aliveness that each of his parents feared, and that they were lost in this new situation, each searching for a program of how to behave in this unanticipated circumstance. David understood that he was a threat to them, not that he was in fact a threat but that he now lived in a fullness of himself that enticed his own parents to move into a place within themselves that they had long ago learned to fear. The place of natural wholeness and aliveness both enticed and threatened them, but this fear was also part of who they had become. David did not know how long he would be able to live here with them again, and besides he longed for the boisterous life of the village, its relaxed ease, and the presence of Grandfather and of Bearman.

Just then he heard a light tap at the door. He thought it was Mother but when he said: "Come in," he was surprised to see Cornelia slink quietly into the room.

"I couldn't sleep," she said. There was an intense glow in her eyes and she seemed full of unexpressed words and thoughts.

David looked at her and he could feel her young mind

stretching and searching, looking for the words that could express something that even she didn't know, but something that longed for answers.

Suddenly she said: "Tell me more about your invisible Elephant."

David realized he must be truthful with her. "Elephant came to me at a time when I was very uncomfortable here at home and also in school."

"I'm also uncomfortable at home," said Cornelia, "sometimes I feel like there is not enough room for me just to be here, that there is not enough air to breathe, and that Mommy and Daddy are uncomfortable with everything I say. I see them kind of flinch when I talk. But I have so looked forward to going to school where I can learn new things and how to read and write."

"I know what you mean about there not being enough room in this house, and with Mother and Father," answered David. "That's the way I felt too. I felt like I was in a cage and I didn't understand why Father said the things to me that he said, or why Mother was always after me to be different. But school was not the solution. School was even more restricted and what I was to do was always determined by the teacher and had very little to do with me. I felt they were trying to turn me into a robot. And I didn't know what to do about it until Elephant came to me."

"Yes! Yes! I knew this is what I needed to hear from you. Tell me about Elephant!"

Elephant

"Elephant was always with me. He would wake me up in the morning with a gentle friendly smile. I always felt that he loved me. Not like Mother or Father but like a dear friend who really cared what happened to me. He was so gentle and he always understood me. And he helped me to know how to be here at home and also at school. And he helped me understand that I had to leave, that I had to leave school and that I had to leave home. He helped me understand that Mother and Father and my teacher, although they did care for me, just wanted me to live in a very limited way, and really didn't want me to change and to grow and to fully become who I am. I always felt that Mother and Father and the teacher all just wanted me to remain a little obedient boy who would do everything they told me to do even if those things had nothing to do with who I am."

"Yes! Yes! Tell me more!"

"Elephant was extremely kind but also very very strong. He knew I needed to be me just like he needed to be an elephant. He told me that elephants have very special talents that no other animal has, not even people, and that it was important for him to learn how to use those talents and to practice them. Because no one else in the world could do it, so that it was his responsibility to develop and use and get to know the talents that were specifically his. That was the job he was given in this world and that each person also has very special talents and qualities that no one else has, and that the only way someone can know this is to discover them for himself. If a person has qualities that no one else has then how could anyone else teach him about them? The only way for him to know them is to go on a journey of discovery and to find them for himself. Elephant taught me that a person is like a treasure hunt and that we may not know where the treasure is hidden but that we have to search for it until we find it and then the treasure itself will help us to know how it is to be used."

"This is the problem I had at home and also at school. People there just wanted me to be like everyone else and to act like everyone else and to do the things that everyone does. But if I did that I would never really get to know myself, I would always see myself only in comparison to everyone else and I would never really get to know my own presence. Elephant taught me that presence is essential and that it is one of the greatest gifts that we have, one of the greatest gifts that any being has. Every animal knows naturally how to be present, but only people learn to hold back their presence and learn not to trust it."

"Yes! Yes! I knew it! I knew it!" Cornelia was overpowered with joy. She felt like she had been waiting all her life to hear these things.

"But there are other things that Elephant taught me and not only Elephant but the real teachers that I have had. We are never alone. We are full of alivenesses of all kinds on the inside. All of life fills us and advises us if we are willing to listen to it and to talk to it. And the aliveness in us calls the aliveness around us, that is how Grandfather knew to come get me and to take me to the place where I could really learn and grow."

"Your Grandfather came to get you???"

"Not Father's father or Mother's father but a wise man who is Grandfather to many people and who also became Grandfather to me. He heard me cry out for a real teacher even though I didn't know that's what I was doing and so he came for me."

"I knew it! I knew it! cried Cornelia. That's why you have come for me!"

David was startled to hear this. He knew he had felt

pulled to come back to this little house where he had first lived but now he was beginning to understand why the pull had been so strong.

The Pull

David didn't know where to begin with Cornelia, or even if he should. He recalled being in the village and telling Grandfather that he was feeling a need to go back home. Grandfather looked at him with that look that went all the way through him, as if Grandfather were seeing something so deep in David that even David didn't know it was there.

"Tell me about this feeling," said Grandfather.

"I have trouble finding the right words for it. I don't want to leave the village, and I know that being here with you and Bearman and all the people in the village is the best thing that has ever happened to me, and still there is this strange feeling deep in my belly that says I should go home. I don't understand it but the feeling is very persistent."

Grandfather's look changed, became wider and warmer, and David felt as if he were being hugged by Grandfather's feeling. He told Grandfather this and Grandfather said: "Yes, it is true. This is a deep call and one that you are listening to even though to your thinking mind it doesn't seem to make much sense. Why don't you talk to this feeling. Maybe it is more than a feeling, maybe it is the energy of some animal inside of you. Ask it if that is so."

By now David was well used to Grandfather's curious ways of teaching. So he closed his eyes and focussed on the feeling and asked: "Are you an animal?"

Immediately a slinky otter appeared behind David's closed eyes. The otter looked at David and suddenly said: "Come swim with me!" and dove directly into the river. David followed without question. He found Otter swimming skillfully against the river's current, winding his way through the various smaller streams that flowed within the river. David realized that the river was not just a single thing, but consisted of many smaller thinner currents, each with its own shape and speed, and the otter was skillfully weaving its way along one of these as if it were a wet path through the river itself. Then it dove through a small underwater opening in the bank of the river, through a short tunnel, and upward into a warm and cozy cave. David followed Otter into this enclosure and then realized that it was Otter's home. In this home cave were two older otters and a younger one. David knew that this was Otter's family. The two older ones came up and sniffed Otter and then David. These were Otter's parents. The younger one came up and joyfully nuzzled Otter and was obviously overjoyed to see him. David told all of this to Grandfather who was sitting by his side and Grandfather said: "Ask Otter if there is anything else."

David did so and Otter shook his head.

Grandfather said: "Thank Otter for guiding you to this knowing and then come back here to me."

David thanked Otter and Otter's family and opened his eyes. Grandfather's eyes were sparkling. "Now you know why you have to go home right now. It is not for you but for someone else who calls you. Perhaps they don't even know they are calling you, just as you didn't know you were calling me when you did, but it is important to pay attention to this call."

Cornelia's Questions

Cornelia was excited about having time with David, she had been longing to ask him questions both about his school and also about something that she was not too sure about; this was his seeming interest in her stuffed animals and dolls. She thought it was unusual for a grown boy to be interested in dolls and stuffed toys. She knew her mother and father showed little interest in them other than to humor her, but she felt that David's interest was deeper and more focussed, although she didn't quite know how to state it. So she asked him: "David, did you have stuffed animals and dolls when you were young? And if you did, where are they now?"

This nudged David out of the thoughts that were running through his mind, thoughts about what was and was not communicated in relationships and how these things balanced each other. So he was not sure that he heard Cornelia correctly and so he asked her: "Do you mean do I still play with toys?"

"No, silly, but maybe that is a good question too."

David gulped and without thinking answered her in a way that surprised even him. "The toys that I had and have are real animals and real people. And what is so important about them is the way you treat them and pay attention to them."

Cornelia felt this conversation going in a direction that she had not anticipated but she also knew that its new direction was more interesting than her original question. So she quickly changed what she had intended to ask. Softly she asked: "How does that happen?" This was something she had learned from her conversations with her mother and particularly with her father. She had learned that if her questions were vague then the answer seemed to be more extensive and also more real.

David looked at her and had to gather his thoughts before he replied. "Toys are like a doorway into your imagination," he heard himself reply although this is not really what he had intended to say. "And the most important thing is to go through this doorway and to learn from the people and the animals that live in your imagination. They are really your deepest friends and teachers."

"I don't know what you mean about the 'doorway.' What do you mean?"

David began to wonder if he was explaining correctly what he knew about this own imagination. "Well, I used to have a friend named Gordy." Again, he was surprised to hear what he was saying. He had never told anyone about Gordy before. "No one else could see Gordy but when I closed my eyes I could see him clearly."

"Why did you close your eyes? I can see Jessie right now even with my eyes open! But I don't see any doorway."

"What about all your dolls and your other toys? Can you see them also?"

"Of course, silly. Can't you?"

"No," said David, somewhat flustered. "I can remember what Jessie looks like but I can't see her the way I used to see Gordy or my friend the Elephant."

"But how could you forget?" Cornelia asked.

"I don't really know," David replied. "For me, I see them much more vividly when I close my eyes. And I remember Jessie, but I don't think I really see her like you do."

"What a strange boy you are. Are boys so different from girls? I think girls can see lots of things and they don't even need to close their eyes."

David began to wonder if perhaps Cornelia was right. He had never considered that someone else's mind might be different from his own. And were girls minds different from boys minds? Were there walls and divisions in his own mind that required doorways but there were no such walls in girls minds? He realized he would have to have long conversations with Cornelia in order to learn what happened inside of her mind.

Cornelia's Council

Sitting in the guest room with Cornelia David suddenly understood why he was there and what Cornelia needed from him.

"There is something else I need to tell you about Elephant," he said. "Elephant was not alone. I met him first as one animal in a circle of animals. So I am wondering if maybe Giraffe is also not alone. Maybe she also is part of a circle. Maybe there are other animals waiting for you to meet them. Close your eyes and call Jessie, ask if she will come to you even though she is still in your own room."

Cornelia was confused, she had always held Jessie while she spoke to her so she didn't know how this would happen now but she trusted David and so she closed her eyes and inside of herself she said: "Jessie, can you come to me now even though you are still in my room?"

Behind her closed eyes Jessie the Giraffe appeared, more vibrant and alive than Cornelia had ever seen her before. Cornelia was astounded. "Jessie, I didn't know you could do that. I thought you were only there when I held you. And you look different, you're not so fluffy and soft but you're strong and alive and really tall!"

Jessie replied: "Of course, I am also soft and small when you need me to be that way, or when I need to be that way with you. But I am also strong and really alive. It's just that you never had a need for me in this way before."

David said: "Ask her if there are also other animals that guide you and if she could take you to them."

Not knowing what to expect, Cornelia asked Jessie: "Are there other animals you could take me to that are here to guide me?"

"There are other animals, and I've been waiting for you to be ready to meet them. Come with me."

Cornelia found herself trailing after Jessie and she had to hurry because Jessie's legs were so long. Suddenly Jessie stopped and said: "Here, climb onto my back and I'll give you a ride." Jessie knelt down on her front knees and lowered her longneck and Cornelia climbed up it until she was on Jessie's back. When Jessie stood up Cornelia was amazed at how high up she was and Jessie trotted off at a quick pace. Walking first through an open savannah Jessie eventually came to a large river and went along the bank until she arrived at a small secluded cove.

Lying partly in the water and partly on the bank was an angry alligator. As Jessie approached Alligator snapped at her. Jessie hesitated and then leaped over Alligator in one bound. Alligator smiled. "He likes to think that this is his place but it belongs to all of us," Jessie said. Cornelia looked around to see who Cornelia meant by "all of us" but all she could see was a large and very old tree. Jessie stopped under the tree and lowered herself onto her front knees so that Cornelia could climb down. Just as Cornelia's feet reached the ground she noticed a very fat snake coiling and uncoiling itself down out of the tree branches. She looked at it and shuddered.

"I don't think I like this place," she said to Jessie. Jessie smiled at her and said: "Snake and Alligator are the primary guardians of the place. Once you get to know them you'll be happy that they are here."

A small squirrel chirped and hopped down out of the tree. Jessie said: "Hello Mr. Squirrel. Look who I've brought to meet you."

Just then a powerful Eagle circled down and landed on the lowest branch of the tree just above them. And as Cornelia looked at Eagle a gentle butterfly with wings of irridescent blue fluttered above and landed on Cornelia's head. She could feel it's soft landing and just then a warmth washed through her entire body. She felt deeply happy and very powerfully present here with these animals under the tree.

Looking around at all of the animals and especially at the tree Jessie said: "This is your council."

Cornelia didn't really understand what Jessie meant as she looked around at the grumpy Alligator, at the slinky and mysterious Snake, at the friendly Squirrel, the powerful Eagle, the warm and gentle and beautiful Butterfly.

"These five animals are my council?"

"Seven!" said Jessie. "Don't forget me here, and you seem not to have noticed this ancient and deeply rooted Tree that provides us all shelter and a place to be. We are the council of advisors that lives within you, that supports you from the inside, and that is here for you. We have been with you even though you didn't know about us, except for me. Why do you think I have been the favorite of all your toy stuffed animals? I was there watching over you and helping to connect you to your own insides, but your insides is much more diverse and unique than you have yet realized. We have been waiting for the time when you would be ready to meet with us so that you can develop a relationship with each one of us and get to know the different qualities of aliveness that have a home inside of you."

Cornelia didn't know what to think, but she felt that in a way she already knew each of these beings and valued them all. She was deeply moved and also exhausted so she bade David good night and retired to her own room and slept the deepest sleep she had ever experienced, but it was warm and cozy and she felt very very good.

David's Dream

During the night David dreamt that he was in a desert. It was a vast and sandy desert, extremely dry, the few trees that occasionally found root in that desert struggled for moisture and had grown deep roots in order to keep from drying up. David was a young boy again, dressed like a desert dweller, hardy, and with heat baked skin, wearing the robes of a desert nomad, and making his way slowly through the surrounding vastness. Occasionally he would meet travelers and they would exchange a respectful greeting but for the most part the desert was devoid of life.

The boy held a secret under his desert tunic, something that he could show to no one, and it was a wooden wand that could show him where moisture was to be found in that vast desert. But this wand also had a special power, and that was that whenever he was lost in the desert the wand could plant itself in the earth and quickly grow deep roots and draw water to the surface from the depths of that parched land. The boy kept the wand hidden from others because he knew that other people would accuse him of witchcraft and rather than using the wand to help make the desert green again, as it had once been long ago, they would destroy the wand as being something wicked and unnatural. The boy wandered through that vast desert always wondering why people refused the very thing that would help them make the desert into a paradise of richness and plenty.

One day as he was making his way through a passage-way between two high cliffs he heard a soft sweet sound, like an almost silent song being sung, and a very small bird flew down to him and landed on his shoulder. He greeted the bird as birds were seldom seen in that dry expanse: "Hello fellow seeker," he said, "wherever have you come from?"

The bird spoke to him in a melodious song, a song that was so soft that it was almost a silent song, and said: "I have come to help you make the desert green again."

"And how will you do that?" asked the boy.

"I don't know," said the tiny bird, "but if you will plant your staff here in the desert and let me take a tiny twig from it I know that the desert itself will show me how, because the desert itself longs to be green again."

The boy felt something stirring deep inside his body and knew he could trust the tiny bird. Gently reaching under his long robe he remove the staff and softly pushed one end into the earth. The earth seemed to open to receive the staff. Still holding it the boy felt a strange vibration and slowly, imperceptively, a tiny branch began to grow from the upper tip. The bird flew down off of his shoulder and taking the new and tender branch in its tiny beak gently pulled until the small branch was freed and the bird flew off into the sky. The boy felt a deep resurgence of warm aliveness and the desert itself shuddered as David woke up.

David lay in bed for a long time steeped in wonder.

Questions

Breakfast time at the house seemed to be full of unanswered questions. But the questions were also unasked. Father, who had said the fewest words since David's return, seemed to be bursting with questions. He felt like a balloon that was ready to explode. Yet he hardly said a word, only "Good Morning!" Mother was busy fixing omelets and toast, coffee, juice, milk, and she had strangely baked a fresh apple pie this morning. Strange because she had never before baked an apple pie for breakfast! She looked lovingly at both David and Cornelia as they sat down to eat while she still scurried around the kitchen, putting more bread in the toaster, getting the butter out of the fridge, and hovering around the table making sure that everything was perfect, but also in this way avoiding the numerous questions that were on her mind. Cornelia sat quietly next to David deeply absorbed in her own thoughts. Only David seemed relaxed and at ease, although he was quietly mulling over the dream that he had had earlier in the morning. In fact, he did not go back to sleep after the dream but had lain in bed letting the dream soak deeply into his thoughts and feelings.

During his time at the village he had learned from Grandfather how to be at home with his dreams. Grandfather had told him that every dream was as unique as a person or an event.

"Dreams are as different as people are, said Grandfather. Only imagine that you are full of different people, each one unique, and each one has something to teach you. You learn something different from each person you meet if you are really alive. If you are not alive you just label them and put them on a shelf and look at them from the outside, like a shelf full of canned goods that you never open. You only look at the labels. What a waste. But if you are really alive then you are thrilled to learn something from each person and from each dream, and you recognize that nothing you learn is the same. Every teaching is different even if at the end they all come together into a giant story. Every dream is a doorway into an event just as every person is a doorway into a relationship. And events and relationships are your greatest teachers. If you are really alive," Grandfather added mysteriously.

David had listened to this in great wonder for he had never really thought about how he had treated people, and he had thought even less about how he had related to his dreams. People were just people and dreams were just dreams but he had never thought that there might be some similarity between people and dreams, or at least his relationship to them. How did he relate to them? And what did Grandfather mean: 'If you are really alive?' What did that mean? Wasn't everyone alive? But as he held this question he knew the answer already. No one seemed as alive to him as Bearman! And Grandfather was really alive but in a different way. In fact, he realized that he had learned very much already from Bearman and from Grandfather but he had learned different things in different ways. And they both seemed so natural in the ways they taught, as if they were just easily hanging out with David being who they were.

So as David sat at the breakfast table he let the dream seep into his pores and let himself feel the vastness of that desert and the beauty of the little bird and the magic of the staff. But he also spoke to the dream, or at least to his dream guide. He had learned from Grandfather that every dream had a guide, like a guide in the mountains, someone who knew the terrain and who could guide you safely on a trek into the beauty and the wonder of the mountains. To the dreamer every dream was a wonder, just like a mountain, but a guide was needed if one were to really see the beauty of the mountain and to climb it and appreciate its uniqueness and not get lost in it. So while David was lying in bed after waking up from the dream he had asked within himself: "Is there a guide that could come to me to guide me into this dream so that I can fully appreciate its beauty as a passageway?"

Immediately a small squirrel had appeared. David knew

this squirrel for he often came when David called for a dream guide. He was always busy, searching for acorns and stashing them in one place or another and he always looked at David with the kindest eyes, eyes that held a deep caring and David had always felt a slight vibration in his chest whenever Squirrel looked at him so deeply.

"Squirrel, this dream feels very beautiful and mysterious to me, can you take me through it so that I can gain the learning and the richness that it brings me?"

Squirrel didn't answer in words but offered David an acorn, for which David thanked Squirrel. David knew from previous meetings with Squirrel that this was the Squirrel's way of saying 'Yes,' but it was also deeper than that. It was a gift that Squirrel offered, and a gift that was part of the way Squirrel survived and stayed alive, so he was really offering David some of his own aliveness. David accepted the acorn with sincere thanks. David had learned that these guides did not always speak the same language as David but that each had his own way of communicating that involved gestures and acts which were perhaps even deeper and more meaningful than words. In fact, communicating with these guides had deepened David's own understanding of himself and of people, for he had come to recognize that communication takes place in different ways and at different levels, and if a person were completely truthful all of these ways would be in harmony, but if the person were confused or in conflict you could feel a disharmony in them. And if a person were deliberately lying then there was something like a clash that you felt deep in your gut. And in these cases what a person did was truer than what a person said.

Squirrel turned around and began to climb a very high tree, and David knew he was to follow him, so he began climbing also, and discovered that he was also a squirrel, and it made climbing much easier for he was light and he had sharp claws that found purchase easily in the tree bark.

Squirrel climbed to the highest branch and there he waited for David to catch up. David asked: "What are we to do here?"

Squirrel waved his paw out over the vastness of the view and David understood he was just to look. From this high vantage point David could see the entire world, not only as it is now but as it had been before it moved into this present moment. He could see the development, and what he saw was a vast wilderness, beautiful in its diversity, and all the various animals. Such an abundance of life! And such an unbelievable variety. All different kinds of birds, from the smallest hummingbirds that were no larger than bees to the giant condors and everything in between, all swooping and hunting and making nests and feeding and sitting on their eggs with great stillness and vigilance, feeding their chicks and eventually helping them learn how to fly, and the chicks growing into adulthood and then raising their own families. Cycle after cycle of caring and growing and changing. And he saw similar scenes for each of the animals: the four-legged creatures (as Bearman and Grand-father called them), the creepy crawlies (the insects), the burrowing worms, snakes with long bodies and no append-ages yet just as skillful as the other animals in their own ways, and the vast hordes of creatures that lived in the seas and oceans. And all the plants and trees and bushes and flowers that grew out of the earth, beings that were rooted and could not walk around, or fly, or swim, or crawl. It was a rich, awesome, creative world, invested with magnificent variety and wonder.

He saw how every kind of life contributed to every other kind of life: the oak trees gave their acorns, plants gave their fruit or seeds, flowers gave their pollen, and ani-mals gave of themselves in order to feed other animals, and when trees died or animals died then hordes of insects began to feed off of these dead creatures, so that even the dead gave of themselves no less than the living. He saw it as a great ball of aliveness, weaving back and forth into itself, renewing itself and thriving. He realized that alive-ness needed aliveness, that no single kind of being could live alone, all beings needed each other.

And he saw that the core of it all, that around which all of this flowing aliveness wove itself, was the earth itself: the land and mountains and rivers and oceans and sky and caves.

And then he began to see something very strange.

Creeping out of the forests and along the waterways and out onto open land was a very strange animal, the human being. This animal moved fast and did something strange along the way. It killed almost everything that it encountered, it removed everything that didn't provide for its own survival, and in its wake it left a barren trail that eventually became the desert, and then the vast desert that David had seen in his dream.

David understood that the desert he had made his way through was the desert of the life that he had encountered at home when he was young and especially in school where anything extraneous was not allowed, only the things that were to be learned, and the words, the language, counting, spelling, reading left almost no room for any other kind of aliveness. He realized that his own culture had created the desert, devoid of the complex and vast aliveness that the earth needed, and he realized that Bearman and Grandfather had seen this void in him, and had helped him to come back to the place where he could honor the time and space needed within himself for the return and renewal of his own wildness, his own complexity and interwovenness, his own wholeness teeming around the earth that he himself was. He understood that the human animal works very hard to create a desert in each of its children, a desert of obedience and a denial of their own vast creative complexity, a place where there is almost no renewal other than that which is judged by the grownups to be good. David realized how dead he himself had been when Grandfather had come to rescue him and how Bearman had helped him come back to his own renewal.

Sitting at the breakfast table David knew why he had come back home.

Father

David was deep in reflection about these musings when Father suddenly spoke but in a voice that David had never heard before.

"David, I am very disturbed about something. I find it very suspicious that MY SON suddenly disappears for five years and then suddenly reappears without any word from him during that time."

"But Father, I did write to you although it wasn't very often, that is true. But my studies kept me so busy that there really wasn't much time to write."

What David said was quite true, he had had very little time to write. His experiences in the village, and with Bearman and Grandfather, had kept him so busy that there was little time for reflection about what was going on in the family that he had left. He was constantly placed in very real situations where he had to rely on his own inherent skills and abilities in order to deal with situations. And the most stressful thing was that initially at least he was in situations where he needed to be constantly alert and extremely present both with the situation and with himself. Grandfather had said that he was being required to return to his own "profound presence" as he had learned to leave it very early in order to follow the patterns that his home and school were requiring of him. Grandfather had said that he had been trained like a dancing bear to leave his own natural rhythm and to dance to a tune that was not his, and that finding and trusting his own rhythm, the rhythm that he was born with, was essential if he was ever going to be fully alive again. So as Father spoke David was keenly aware that Father himself was out of rhythm, that he was following a pattern or playing a role that had nothing to do with the present situation, that Father was acting as he thought others expected him to act rather than being profoundly present with himself.

Mother and Cornelia were both shocked at Father's harsh words. Father seemed to be looking for someone to blame, and also for a way to discharge his own anger, but an anger that had nothing really to do with the present situation.

David just looked at Father calmly and remembered his dream of the vast desert. He had the feeling that Father was wandering around in that desert himself looking for some stray element of aliveness.

"There is life in that desert, Father!"

Father was shocked to hear David say this and he felt suddenly very off balance. David's reply had nothing to do with what Father had just said so he was unprepared for his own experience and for a moment didn't know even where he was. David had really spoken to a place where Father often felt himself to be, a place almost completely devoid of life, a place of wandering aimlessly in search of his own aliveness, yet a place he had avoided looking at for most of his life. Father had spent his time avoiding his own aliveness yet at the same time searching for it. His only place of safety was to retreat into roles and patterns that had been developed early in his life but that had very little to do with what was going on in the present moment. The terror of being lost and of admitting it to himself and to others was always just beneath the surface of his awareness.

Mother and Cornelia both watched as Father's skin turned eerily white and he suddenly fell off his chair gasping for breath. They rushed to Father but David had already picked him up and was holding him and gently rocking him in his arms.

The Rhythm of Aliveness

As David held Father tenderly in his arms David felt around for Father's rhythm. In his work with Grandfather and Bearman David had learned to trust his own rhythm, and to always return to it whenever he felt out of tune or off key in some way. Now he was very strongly immersed in his own rhythm and at the same time he was feeling around for Father's real rhythm. He felt the strong pulse of his own and immediately next to it was the almost mechanical and harsh beat of the rhythm that Father had taken on early in his life. David felt it like a brick wall that was strong and protective, and David gently leaned into that wall with his own lively rhythm. David understood that one's own rhythm was a gift from the Great Spirit of the Universe and that one was given this gift and it was intended to carry one through the journey that we call life. In the village David had learned that the rhythm never ends but eventually must return to that great Orchestra out of which we have all come, but that while we are here it is the gift that we carry and that also carries us as we make this mysterious journey of discovering why it is that we have been sent here.

As David leaned gently into that strange brittle wall that Father carried as a rhythm the wall began slowly to give way and although it didn't crumble as David had thought it might instead it melted enough to let David's rhythm squeeze through.

David was not prepared for what he experienced on the other side.

A tiny baby was squealing and moving frantically, crying out to be fed. But there was no one else in sight. The baby was needing dreadfully to be fed and changed and warmed, to be held and loved, but no one was there. David experienced that the tiny being felt abandoned and lonely and uncared for and cried and cried until it fell asleep exhausted. A few moments later a woman came in and picked baby up carrying him into the next room. "The doctor says to just let him cry when he is like this or else he will learn that he is in control rather than us, Dear. I don't like hearing him cry so much but I know that the doctor knows best." As the baby awakens this woman quickly stuffs a bottle in his mouth before he can begin to cry again.

As David watches this scene he feels the sting of emptiness and the lack of relationship, the lady is following a set of rules that are not even her own and is treating the baby as if it were a mechanical thing. This is so very different from the warmth and caring that David had felt in the village. There he had learned that everything is always in relationship with everything else, always, and that a part of the path one is here to walk is to be aware of that relationship and to be available to it. David could feel the deep terror that his father had always carried with him and the brittleness of the patterns that Father had used in order to wall off that same terror.

David's own rich rhythm moved over toward that baby and gently took it from the woman who was holding it. He knew that the baby had very early been jarred out of its own natural rhythm and forced to fit a different rhythm, but it wasn't even a human rhythm that it had learned to fit itself to, but the mechanical rhythm of a set of wordy rules that were very distant from the natural aliveness of that tiny being. As David held the tiny baby he felt into it for its own rhythm. He could feel his own rhythm embracing that tiny little rhythm, warming it, loving it, valuing it, just as the mother Eagle feels the rhythm inside each of the eggs she is brooding and values it as her own.

David held that tiny being and rocked it until it could come out of its own terror and feel the warmth and caring of the larger surrounding rhythm. Then it let itself relax and return to letting its own rhythm pulse louder and louder from within.

Just then Father slowly opened his eyes. He had been

crying. "What happened? I just had the most incredible dream," he said. "I dreamt that I was an important being and that the entire Universe was holding me, and I could see Jesus, and Mary was crying because he had been killed, but then he returned from the dead, just as the Bible says, and He spoke to me: 'Just love,' He said, 'just love!' When I heard his words and felt his presence I just cried and cried. Halleluja!"

Being Stuck

David was not surprised to hear Father's exclamation. From his years of living in the village he had learned that the non-native culture had a practice of trying to find a place where one could fasten oneself in a secure manner. And that it didn't seem to matter much what one was tied to as long as it could be spoken and was predictable.

"The people we rescued you from particularly like the things they call books, and there is one specific book that they seem to stick to more than any other. They call it 'The Book,' or the Bible." Grandfather had a grin on his face a he spoke to David. "They learn some stories from this book and then tell them over and over again and force their children to tell the same stories and as long as everybody tells the same stories they seem to be happy. In fact, when they first came to our land the thing they tried to force on us was to tell their stories. They didn't seem to understand that we had our own stories, and that our stories were very alive, not frozen on some leaves in The Book! We understood that they had a history of even killing people who did not tell the same stories that they did, or of killing people who told the stories differently, even though they were the same story. We thought they were truly insane in the way they insisted that we say the same words that they did. They didn't care to understand our words or our stories but they thought that their stories were more valuable than someone's life. One of the things that we love best is to hear the stories that children tell, for they are always fresh and alive. They are like new green shoots that grow out of the earth in the springtime, and we delight in their blossoms. We always wonder what color they are going to be and we delight in this garden of our children's stories. But we saw that the invaders were very harsh with their own children, and made them hurt if they told their stories differently from the grownups. Eventually their children did learn to tell their stories but in a very brittle frozen way that did not leave room for their own aliveness. We felt that was cruel and stupid of those parents."

"Eventually the invaders forbid us to tell our own stories, and to do the dances and the ceremonies that were part of the stories. They had their marks on the special leaves that they brought with them, and they would show them to us to 'prove' that our stories were forbidden. We didn't understand how they could be so stupid. We saw that they were frozen into their stories, that they were stuck in them the way an animal sometimes gets stuck in mud when it is too deep and we felt that we had to help free them from this mud just like we would any other animal. But when we tried it they really got angry and called us foul names that we didn't understand. We had no idea why they were so angry but then we heard from one of them that they had had to leave their own country because in their original homes other peoples stories didn't fit with theirs and so they had to leave to go to a place where they could tell their stories freely. But we thought that should make them more tolerant of our stories but it seemed to do just the opposite. They had become as rigid as those who had forced them away from their own original lands."

"So we learned very quickly to see the places where they were stuck in their own patterns. And we came to understand that they thought it was a great gift to be stuck there. They didn't seem to know that their frozenness kept them from being fully alive, and they seemed then to fear people who were alive. The curious thing was that they thought their stuckness was intelligent. We could see how it limited them. The thing that saddened us most though was the way they forced their children to be stuck just as they were."

"And that is why we felt it was so important to heed your call and to come rescue you before they could freeze you. We could feel that you longed to be fully alive. We could feel your struggles all the way here and that is why I took the long trip to help you escape from that imprisonment."

Frozen Thinking

"If you are not supposed to be stuck anywhere, then where are you supposed to be?" David had asked Grandfather at that time. But he could also feel that the natural answer to his question already existed somewhere within himself, if he could only get to it.

Grandfather had stared at David for a long time before he replied, and David felt a strange sensation in his body, like a soft tingling, while Grandfather looked at him. Finally Grandfather answered, and the answer both shocked David and it also felt like it gathered him together in a certain inexplainable way.

"Every person is essentially free," Grandfather had said. "But most people have learned to be afraid of that freedom. Every person is free to travel to journey, to wander."

As he said this David reflected on how he had travelled away from home with Grandfather, into this village at the border of the mountains and the sea. To people that he had not previously known where he felt so deeply free. But at the same time he was remembering the home where he had grown up with its rules and the expectations of his parents, expectations where he didn't feel free but felt like he had to do things for the sake of his parents. And he also remembered the school where he was not free at all, but had to sit in a room, in a certain place, and his time was regulated not by what he enjoyed doing but by what someone else told him to do almost every moment that he was there. In school he had not felt free at all. But while David was in this reverie Grandfather had continued talking, although seeming to wait for David to bring his awareness back to him. And what he said startled David.

"Every person is free within himself. If you observe yourself closely you will realize that right now you had gone into a memory that you have brought here with you. You didn't realize it but I could also see that memory that you brought here. Maybe not exactly as you saw it, but I could sense the energy in it and how it grabbed you. And I saw that you left being present with me here and wandered off. Of course you were free to do that but you did not go there freely; the memory itself grabbed you and carried you off."

David was truly shocked. He had never before thought of things grabbing him and carrying him away.

"Some people live most of their lives there, grabbed by things and trapped in them so that they no longer have the freedom to wander everywhere. What a limited life that would be, don't you think so?"

David had to agree with him.

"And that is the place from which I went to rescue you! You were on the verge of being trapped and imprisoned in just such a place for the rest of your life. And you and your animals were crying out to the Universe for your rescue!"

David felt the terror of the direction that he was really on the edge of going into at the time when Elephant had told him he had to leave school, and he had realized that he would also have to leave home, but he had also not known just how he would do that. And just then Grandfather had appeared in the nick of time.

Grandfather had laughed and said, "Just think, right now you would be a prisoner wearing the uniform of prison stripes if you had not managed to escape. Your community was trying to confine you into your thinking, and into a particular way of thinking, into specific thoughts that would have repeated over and over again for the rest of your life. You would have carried your own prison within yourself and have been trapped in it and the whole time thinking that you were free. For that is also one of the thoughts that you would have repeated over and over again: that you lived in the freest country in the world." At this point Grandfather almost doubled over in laughter. David felt a shiver run through him, recognizing the truth of what Grandfather had said.

"Thinking needs to be free to go wherever it needs to go for it is one of the leading edges of our search for freedom. How can it do that if it is trained like a monkey and free to go only in the directions that are already frozen into it. What kind of freedom is there in a deep freeze?" Grandfather laughed and laughed at his own joke although David again felt a shiver run through himself.

"Yes, the people you came from prepare their children for consumption and their children don't even know that they will be eaten!"

Mother

"Of course, most people don't realize that their thinking is stuck. They think that their thinking is true. But that is just more thinking. Stuck thinking about thinking just goes around in circles. And justifies its own existence," Grandfather continued. "Thinking should be free and wild, like the forest and the sea, but people have learned to think that wildness is dangerous. Wildness is deeply intelligent and was meant to be free. But wildness respects wildness and most people have lost that respect, especially for their own wildness."

David had listened with rapt attention. He was hearing something that deep within himself he already knew, but he had never realized. "Can a person know something and at the same time not know it?" he had asked Grandfather.

"The people you came from think that knowing depends on learning. For us 'wild' people, knowing depends on going deeply into oneself where things are already known. Your people have confused training with knowing. But their kind of training freezes a person. What you will do here with us is to go deeply into who you are and to gather yourself together and as you do you will find that you grow larger and larger and become freer and freer. But you need someone to wake you up when you get stuck. Bearman is one of the best at waking people up. Because he is completely at home in his own wild awakeness."

David immediately liked the words 'wild awakeness.' He felt something stirring down in his belly when he heard them. "Yes," he said, "at home I felt like a tamed dog. Going out into the forest with Bearman I have come to relish something in my body that loves the thrill of not knowing what will happen. And Bearman has already helped me to see that my body knows how to do things that I didn't think were possible."

"Yes, thinking 'thinks' that it is supposed to know everything before it happens. What a dull life that would be," replied Grandfather. "And how much time is wasted on 'learning' when our real job is to discover in ourselves the things we already know. And they are vast, vast. But your people think everyone should be the same, and we are not, not at all. Each person is uniquely different. Uniquely and vastly different, but how would we know that if we all try to be the same?"

David could see himself sitting in the schoolroom with everyone reading the same thing, doing the same lessons, answering the same questions, as if they were parts being produced in a factory. It had been so different from his life in the village, going on a different adventure each day, and talking freely about it to Bearman or Grandfather, and them listening with rapt attention to his stories. David realized that no one in his previous life had paid so much close attention to him and really listened to what he had to say. Here he felt deeply nurtured and cared for, like never before.

Now, sitting at the breakfast table with Father, Mother, and Cornelia, David realized that this was also an adventure, a great adventure and he also realized how predictable Father and Mother were, and also how timid and afraid they were, but Cornelia was a different matter. He could feel that there was a large amount of wildness in her and that she needed someone to talk to who could understand her and not try to make her into someone that she wasn't. She needed someone to really listen to her stories of her adventures.

Father had hurried off to work. He seemed to be relieved that he could leave. David felt what a threat he was to Father, that Father had no ready pattern that he could fall into when confronted with David's wide presence and the safest thing he could do was to avoid and escape, which he did to great relief.

Mother was another matter. She really wanted to get to know David again and she instinctively felt what a large and beautiful young man he was now. She was thrilled and proud of who he had become, and could herself identify with his free presence, but she also felt a certain responsibility to continue to shepherd him as she had always done when he was young. But she also felt clumsy and uncomfortable about how to be with him. She realized she felt like a young schoolgirl with her first crush on a boy. And this was completely in conflict with everything she thought about what being a mother should be. So even though she wanted to stay and spend time with him she readied herself to go out.

"Come, Cornelia, we need to go shopping. We don't have enough food in this house to feed such a big handsome young man." She blushed as she said this.

"No, Mommy, I'll stay home and visit with David."

Mother was unprepared for such a distinct, forceful and independent answer from Cornelia. She became flustered and fumbled around with the keys to the car, and wanted to both stay and run away at the same time.

"Well, then. I'll be back in a jiffy."

66

Jiffy was a word she hadn't heard herself say since she had been in high school, and was herself surprised to hear it.

David's strong voice seemed to clear the air for her. "Mother, we'll be fine. Don't let me interrupt the things I know you need to do."

So Mother left feeling a great sense of relief but also a longing to stay with her new grown son.

David felt a deep sorrow for his mother. He saw clearly the cage of thinking that she was trapped in and also her longing to be free in her own aliveness. He could feel her struggling at the boundary of her own ideas about who she was and who she should be.

Interactive Realities

Cornelia and David were delighted to be left alone together. They both felt they had much to talk about and they were also fascinated to hear each other's stories. They knew they couldn't talk in front of Mother or Father because they knew both had their restrictive orientations where they were so ready to pounce and to criticize and not understand. David felt Cornelia's hunger to know things from him, and he was also interested to hear how things had been for Cornelia. He sensed that she had remained very open and free rather than trying to be obedient as he had been. But he had also discovered that being obedient had put him in a smaller and smaller cage. At least until he met Elephant and the other animals. They had helped him escape into a place where he could trust his own growing rather than it being ordered by a grownup. But now he himself was a grownup, in fact he felt more mature than his own parents.

"Cornelia, I'm very interested to hear the stories you have to tell about your life here at home and in this town. I feel it has been very different from the way my life was when I lived here."

"Oh, your life away at this special school sounds very interesting and that is what I would like to hear. I want to hear your stories. I'm sure they are much more interesting than mine."

"I do want to share them with you, and I know that you realize they were a bit different from how I tell them to Mother and Father," David answered. "But I also really want to know how your life has been here with our parents. When I lived here I found Father difficult to talk to. He had his own understanding of almost everything I said and he didn't seem to hear me at all. It felt to me like he listened to his own thoughts rather than to what I was saying. And Mother was very bossy, always telling me what to do and what I did that was wrong. It wasn't anything big, just about getting up in the morning and getting to school on time and tidying up my room, and all that."

"Oh, Dad is really an old softy," Cornelia replied. "He'll do anything I say if I say it right. He's also the same way with Mom. I watch her and learn what I need to say to get him to do things my way. He's not at all the way you describe him. You just didn't know how to talk to him. And Mom is so afraid of everything, she's always careful and cautious and worried. She's always wondering what the neighbors will think and what people will say about what she does. It sounds to me like you and I really had different parents!"

David was surprised to hear this. He had not thought about the possibility that who his parents were, that is, how they behaved, depended on who they were with. It sounded like they had been one way with him and a very different way with Cornelia. During his time with them David had grown so used to Bearman and Grandfather just being who and how they were, regardless of who was around. He felt they were really centered in themselves and that self was available to whoever was around them, and that this is how he had wished to grow, whereas he now saw that who Mother and Father were was very dependent on who they were with. They were one way with him and another way with Cornelia, and he had only now seen them with both him and Cornelia together. But there was something else that was tugging at him. He recognized that the things he had told Mother and Father about his school were put into words especially for them. He had not been completely open and expressive with them, but had tailored his words to suit them and the way he thought they would understand because he thought they would not understand, that they would be completely upset to hear that he had actually run away from home and that the story of being chosen by the governor for a special school had actually been a lie to protect himself from a barrage of questions and to protect them from being hurt by what he had done. Had he learned to protect them from himself and him from them? And how long had this been going on? Was that just something happening now or had that been going on all his life with them? Had he adapted to their own protective patterns all his life and participated in them? Where exactly was the dividing line between his actions and their expectations, and had this been one of the ways that he had imprisoned himself all along? He was full of jumbled questions and knew he would have to spend some time alone in order to come to the bottom of this.

David was very aware that both Grandfather and Bearman had no expectations, and were just direct with him in how they were and in what they said to him. There was no subterfuge on their part. Yet he was discovering now that he and his parent seemed to have always played a game of being relatively false with each other. That they had expectations of each other and communicated what and how the other wanted to hear. The freedom that he had felt in the village came from not trying to fulfill other people's expectations. He was free to just be who he was. He realized that in the village he did not feel at all judged by other people, but at home he felt constantly judged.

Musing on this he then asked Cornelia: "How do Mother and Father expect you to be?"

"I never think about that," she answered. "I just am. What a silly question."

David reflected to himself: Maybe he was as responsible for how they were with him as they were. Maybe it was like a game that they played with each other, and this game was part of the falseness of their presence with each other.

More Questions

David began to realize that the world was not as he had construed it. Although he had grown mightily into his own being while living in the village with Bearman and Grandfather, there were things he needed to learn also about the world that he had left behind and now returned to. Perhaps this was why Grandfather had suggested to him that it was now time to return to his original home for a while.

He was beginning to realize that he was here to learn from Cornelia, although initially he had begun to think that he was returning in order to help her grow in the way he had. But if her world was so different from the way his had been it was necessary to know this. Also, she seemed to be very whole, much more whole than he had been at that age, much more in contact with the way things were at home, and she knew her way around. She could speak clearly and she was highly perceptive. Perhaps they were to teach one another; he to teach her about his life in the village with Bearman and Grandfather, and she to teach him

73

about the world that she lived in here at home. He could see that her world was quite different from the way his had been even though the setting seemed to be the same. And the next thought quite surprised him: was it possible that even though he had had to leave school and home in order to fully develop into himself, was it also possible that some people really did need home and school in order to do the same thing? This last question began to shake the firmness of the understanding that he had grown into. He realized that he would have to reevaluate where he was even though he had grown strong and secure. Perhaps there was much value in the world he had left behind when he had driven off with Grandfather. In his certainty and security he was beginning to feel just a bit uncertain.

Grownup Children

Cornelia interrupted his ruminations with a sudden question. "Why did you leave and why have you come back?"

David was startled to hear such direct and almost demanding words from such a young girl.

David answered her question with a question of his own: "Aren't you glad that I've come back?"

"Yes, of course," answered Cornelia, "but that's not what I'm asking you."

Again, David was taken aback at her directness, and he was also aware that his first answer to her was an attempt to avoid really looking at what he should say to her. For one thing he felt she was too young for him to answer her truthfully, on the other hand he had learned from Grandfather that almost always a direct and honest answer was the best and clearest thing. Furthermore, he liked her curiosity and he appreciated her directness. Perhaps she was more grown up than he had been at that age. And the only respectful thing to do was to answer her openly and honestly and to see where it led.

"I have difficulty with your questions because for one thing I think you may be too young to hear my answers."

Again, her reply startled him: "How old do I have to be in order for you to tell me the truth?"

With questions and answers like hers he knew he had no choice but to be as honest and direct as she was being. "I have to apologize to you. You have made me aware that I have been treating you like a child but your words aren't those that I could have asked when I was your age. You seem to be much older than I was when I was five years old. So I have to respect the questions you ask and tell you that I feel a bit uncomfortable answering them, but I will."

"Great!" Cornelia almost yelled. "Finally someone who can answer me directly when I ask something. Mother and father are so evasive when I ask them difficult questions. They don't seem to understand that I enjoy thinking about things. It gets so tiring trying to wrestle with them in order to get an honest answer. They don't think I know when they're lying. And they don't seem to realize that I really do want to know things. I used to ask them about you and they never wanted to answer me directly but always talked about what a good boy you are and how smart you are and that you had to go to a special school. Now that you're here I want to know directly from you because I have all kinds of questions saved up that were never answered."

David took a deep breath. The growing that had begun with Grandfather and Bearman in the village seemed to him to be continuing here at home with his little sister. Only he was having difficulty thinking of her as little. Her questions were so direct and challenging that he started to realize that her mind was very mature even at her young age. And he began to wonder if maybe his own mind was also mature at a young age, but that he had acceded to his parents view that he was too young. Could it be that he had been treated like a child and so he had learned to act like one? For he realized he had always had a yearning to grow and to evolve and to be fully whoever he was. Through Cornelia's questions he was realizing that perhaps a mind is born mature and that it learns quite skillfully to be infantile. With this realization he began to see his own parents in an entirely new light. Maybe they were still being the children they had learned to be even though their bodies were that of grownups!

What if parents are really children trying to act like they think grownups are supposed to act? Such a thought suddenly startled him. But this would be only an act, like putting on a play and pretending they were mature when they really weren't.

David began to recognize that this had been exactly his difficulty when he had decided to leave school and to run away from home. School had been training him to put on an act of being intelligent but he had realized that what he longed for was to really grow up. Only Grandfather and Bearman had helped him to do this. And in many ways they were very childlike: direct, honest, questioning, and humorous. And they had really liked David, in fact they had felt a deep love for one another. David realized that his parents and his teachers had always felt uncomfortable with his honest questions, and in fact, they had evaded them just as he himself had begun to evade Cornelia's questions. So he realized that what Cornelia really needed from him was forthrightness and complete honesty.

Conversations with Cornelia

David's thoughts and realizations about grownups was suddenly interrupted by Cornelia: "So, answer my question: what was your school like, and also, why are you so reluctant to tell me about it?"

David was taken aback by Cornelia's vocabulary. She was using words that he didn't even know when he was her age.

Just now I was realizing that our parents are really children who are putting on an act of being adult. But I am also seeing that you are very adult especially for your age and I don't know how that could happen.

"Very early I learned that our parents use words in order

to try to control, not only to control me but to control each other as well. And I began to wonder, what are these strange noises that we call words. And why would people want to control other people. I initially tried to ask Mom and Dad these questions but they only became confused and tried even harder to control me. They were really afraid of my questions so I began asking my questions not to them but just inside of myself. I would ask the question silently and just let the question begin to work in its own way."

"How do you mean, to let the question work in its own way?" David asked.

"Well, something in me really wanted to know. But I realized that the knowing was not going to come from Mom or Dad, not the real knowing anyway. Their answers were often just ways of avoiding my questions and that was frustrating. So I understood that they didn't want me to know, or else they were scared of my knowing, or maybe they themselves were scared of knowing what I was asking. So I had to ask my questions and then just watch. And since their answers were not really answers but ways of running away from answering my questions just became more and more silent questions. I still asked them but not out loud. And my questions then helped me to be aware, and showed me that if I waited and watched then I would understand the answer."

David was overwhelmed by the complexity of this

answer from such a young child. He understood that there was a beautiful clarity in Cornelia, that she had learned to see people clearly and not only through their words and what they said but also through what they didn't say. She was not confused by their words the way he had been as a child, but saw that she had understood early on that words were a kind of mask that many people wore. And he remembered the dances in the village when the night was dark and only fires were burning and the dancers came out in masks, masks of animals, or of demons and ogres, or of other people, but inside the mask was always something else. He realized that Cornelia had also seen the dance that people do, and that the masks they wore were masks of words and language, and that if you understood they were wearing masks you could also realize that there was a real person inside the mask, and that his parents were doing a dance without even realizing they were dancing rather than being real.

And David also understood something very profound: Cornelia was very very real!

Real Talks

David began: "It is so refreshing to hear and see how clear you are. It was this lack of clarity that caused me to run away in the first place."

"You ran away??? Mom and Dad always said you had gone off to a special school!"

"It was a special school, a very special school, but not the kind of school that I had been used to or that Mother and Father know about. This was a school where I was in very real situations where I had to act and be aware and to learn from what I did in each moment. It was not at all like the school I went to here in this town, a school where I just had to obey and to answer questions and do whatever the teacher said."

"Wow! I want to hear all about it. It sounds like something I would love."

"I'm sure you would love it, but you are way ahead of me. When I was your age I believed whatever anyone told me. But luckily I had Gordy and Elephant who always told me the truth. In fact, it was Elephant who told me that if I didn't leave school I would be put in a cage and could never escape. I understand now that you have escaped that cage, the cage of believing the words of other people."

"Lots of times I don't even believe my own words," Cornelia replied, much to David's surprise. "To me words are like clothes. You try on clothes to see if they fit and to see how they feel and to see if you like the colors. Lots of times they don't fit, or they don't feel right. And I certainly don't go around trying on other people's clothes. I let them wear them and I wear my own, but I don't go around showing them off. Lots of people like to parade around in their word-clothes and try to force them on other people. I see Mom and Dad do that all the time."

David could hardly believe his ears that such wisdom could come from such a small girl, but he was beginning to understand that Cornelia was a very special being and he was already learning from her. David said, "but I see that you like to ask a lot of questions so you must want to hear what other people have to say."

"I let my questions take me to answers in their own way, either through people or around people, and I know that people use words in strange ways. But this is the first time that I've heard that words form cages for people," Cornelia replied.

"Grandfather taught me that people first of all use word-cages to hide in so that other people won't hurt them or so that others will like them, but after a while they find that they can't get out of those cages and can't even see them any more. It's when the cages are invisible that people are really trapped and they feel caught in something but don't know what it is. That's when they believe that if they get other people to live in the same cages they will feel freer."

"I like thinking that we have a grandfather!" Cornelia almost yelled in joy.

"He's not really our grandfather, that's just what everyone in the village called him."

"Oh, I see. Those are just the clothes he wore for other people."

"Yes, in a way, but it was also a way that people showed their respect to him."

"Why was he respected? What did he do?"

"He kind of kept an eye on what was going on in the village. He knew everyone and could feel if they were in any sort of trouble or conflict, and he went out of his way to help people understand and live in warmth and harmony with others. In a beautiful sort of way he was the grandfather of the entire village. And he came to rescue me. He heard my call when I knew I needed to leave school and this home."

"You must have called real loud!" Cornelia said with a smile.

"I didn't say a word other than to Elephant, but Grandfather heard my feelings and my desperation. He knew things that were independent of distance. And when he did something he did it without any doubt. He just knew things without being able to explain them to others and he trusted his knowing. But his knowing was deeper than words and it was this kind of knowing that he knew I needed in myself."

"I know that place," Cornelia suddenly blurted out,

"and I feel that I know Grandfather also even though you have barely mentioned him. It's like trying on word-clothes. There's a place that knows whether they fit or not and that place is deeper than the words themselves. And Grandfather feels very very real to me even though I have never met him. And I know that some day I will."

The Village

"So tell me about this village where you lived, the one that Grandfather was the grandfather of," Cornelia continued.

"Well, everyone in the village knew everyone else. And they all helped each other whenever there was anything that needed to be done, especially if it needed to be done quickly. Many of the people lived together in a very big house that had only one big room. That's where I slept, but other people and other families slept there too."

"You mean you didn't even have your own room?"

"Well, it wasn't so necessary to have your own room there. There was lots of space around the village where you could go if you needed to be alone, and all the space was part of the village and everyone used it whenever they needed to. There were mountains all around one side of the village, and there was an ocean along the other side, with coves and beaches, with fishing places and pools for swimming. And the mountains and the ocean were very wild so going anywhere was always an adventure. I loved going into the forest where I learned on my first day there that it was better if you wore no clothes."

"No clothes? Wasn't that weird? What if someone saw you?"

"First of all, the people in the village weren't concerned about nakedness. They felt it was normal for people to enjoy being naked and there was nothing forbidden or secret about it. Everyone has a body and I learned there to respect my own body and the bodies of other people, and not to intrude, not even by looking and certainly not to stare. This seemed to be the basis of a deeper respect that the people had for each other, respect for dreams that they had, or for their imagination, and also for mistakes they made. In a certain sense, people were clothed in respect and that was much finer than any clothes you could wear."

"Secondly, being naked in the mountains or in the sea felt delicious. You could feel all of nature with your body, and I came to realize that nature is also naked, and that when we wear clothes we are kind of hiding ourselves from nature, from the other animals, from the trees and the plants and the flowers. They like to smell us as much as we like to smell them. And the animals seemed to trust me much more if I was naked. Wearing clothes in the mountain came to feel like I was hiding myself in some way."

"And besides that, my skin came to feel much more alive. I realized that my body knew lots of things, like seeing with your skin, and knowing what was present all the way around you."

"But didn't you get cold?"

"After I got used to it being cold wasn't something to be avoided. It actually felt good and sparkling and alive. Of course if it was dangerously cold we had blankets and furs we could wear but that was only when it was close to freezing. And these were the blankets and skins that we also slept in so they began to feel like friends rather than like something that hung in a closet."

"It sounds really exciting and different. I would love it but I can't imagine Mom and Dad being able to live there. They have so many rules about everything. We can't even be naked here in our own house. Even when it's real warm and I feel like just wearing my panties or my pajamas, Mom always says, 'Put something on, what if someone came to the door?' She seems to be really scared of what might happen, especially if it involves other people. I could never understand why she is so focused on people who aren't even here. Was she that way when you lived here?"

"Oh, yes. She was more aware of what could possibly happen than she was of what was going on right now, and it always seemed like she was surrounded by people who weren't here, and she was really concerned about what they might think. In the village people were very present with whatever was happening right then and there, and they might think about possibilities, but they realized that these were just their thoughts rather than something that was really going to happen. They were profoundly present rather than lost in their thinking. But they were also very open and honest with each other. And they laughed a lot. They seemed to always find something funny to laugh about. And they also loved to play. Grownups here don't play. They might go to a game and watch someone else play but it always seemed to be much more serious than playing to them. In the village people could play spontaneously as well as being serious when that was needed. Looking back right now I see that the people in the village seemed to be much more alive than anyone in this town had been."

"It sounds like great fun," said Cornelia wistfully. "When can we go there?"

The Cage of Thinking

Just then Mother returned and David and Cornelia were surprised that it was already noon. They were not aware that any time had passed, and they looked at each other strangely when Mother asked what they had been doing all morning.

"We've just been talking," Cornelia answered. "David told me all about the vill…the school where he lived."

David looked curiously at Cornelia and then at Mother.

"Yes, we would like to hear more about your school also when Daddy arrives," Mother said. It was strange to hear his mother call his father "Daddy," it sounded so childish. He didn't remember ever having heard her call him that before.

"Yes, I'll tell you all about it," David answered nervously, not really knowing what he was going to say to them. He knew he couldn't talk to them as openly as he had to Cornelia about the village, but Mother also gave a hint of being in no hurry to hear about it. He felt she was divided. Part of her was very curious about where he had been and a part of her was terrified to hear about his adventures. He felt she really wouldn't have a place within herself for the story he might tell, and that there was no room in her that could accommodate his new self. She was juggling her understanding about this new mature stranger that she should know, after all, she had given birth to him and he had lived with her for eleven years of his life, but he was now too big and "other" for him to have a place within the ideas she had about what the world was like.

Cornelia also noticed the quickness of her movements and of her statements, as if she were hurrying herself in order not to have to stretch her mind in an unknown way in order to be able to house a new and strange story in it, a story that she would have difficulty telling her friends and neighbors. She was trying to fit David into the story he had occupied before in her thinking but he would no longer fit, and it would be terrifying to stretch her story of who she was in order to have room for this strange man now. Cornelia suddenly understood the cage of thinking that David had spoken about and saw clearly how her mother was trapped in it. And a curious idea popped into her head about how she could help.

"His school was called The Village," Cornelia said, addressing her mother. "And it was a model of the way community might evolve. He was studying possible ways people might live together in a crowded world."

David was shocked; first of all at the way Cornelia used words so skillfully, and secondly at the bright idea he could see she was developing. David saw immediately that Cornelia knew the map of ideas in which mother lived, and that she was using words that would fit into their mother's map of reality, so that she would not have to stretch her perspective very much in order to understand a short story of where David had been for the past five years.

"Yes," added David, "it was a model for a futuristic school."

Mother nodded and looked relieved, and it was obvious that she had heard enough for the moment in order to be at ease.

David suddenly recalled Grandfather's meeting with the principal of his school when he first arrived to take David to the village and Grandfather's answer when David had asked him what he had said to the principal: Your principal is a minor functionary, a cog in a system that is frozen. All I needed to do was push a few buttons in his thinking and he filled in the blanks. He was totally confused and was struggling to hold his thinking together so it would make sense the way it always had to him.

Mother Again

David was rather surprised that Mother had not asked more questions now that the topic of his school had been opened by Cornelia. He had thought that she would be curious to hear every detail, but she actually seemed relieved to have these few bits of information that Cornelia has supplied; that seemed to be sufficient for her. Or was it perhaps that having some information she really didn't want to know more. The information she had was safe information and she didn't want to hear things that would be difficult for her to package into her already organized thinking? David had never before recognized what a rigid woman his mother actually was. And he was flooded with questions about her: Where was her curiosity? Where was her interest? Where was her spontaneous aliveness?

David had grown so used to having people around him in the village that were beautifully alive and responsive. People who could joke and play and be fully present as well as being able to seriously discuss whatever was happening. David was recognizing what a bleak home he had left, and how full the village was of vital people who always helped him remain profoundly present. He was beginning to feel that his mother and father were in fact half dead and limited to a world of fixed thinking that had been cast years before, in fact, frozen long before he had been born. Had he actually been born into a dead world? A world killed by the repeated thinking that people had learned and just repeated over and over? Where was their aliveness? Did they not miss it? Or had it been buried for so long that it was actually threatening when it began to show itself? He realized now that his return was very threatening to his own parents.

Only Cornelia was really alive and profoundly present to him. How had she managed to survive in her aliveness living with parents that were so dead?

But another thought quickly entered his mind. He began to realize that he had also been very dead when Grandfather had rescued him! And that Bearman and Grandfather and the people in the village had helped him to return to his own aliveness, an aliveness that he had not even realized had been severely limited by the world that he had grown up in here at home. And how many children were actually born into a world that was not really alive, and to which they were required to sacrifice their aliveness in order to perpetuate the patterns of that dead and predictable world? What was the tradeoff? What was so valuable to the children that they were willing to sacrifice the thing that he had begun to realize was the most precious thing in the world, their own aliveness?

The Trade

That same evening, after Father had returned from work and the family had eaten their evening meal almost in silence but with the usual small talk that he remembered so well, his parents had retired to the living room to watch the evening news on TV. David and Cornelia remained in the kitchen, having offered to wash and dry the dishes, and David had spontaneously asked Cornelia, "Do you watch the news also?" David remembered having watched the evening news with Mother and Father but finding it either shocking or extremely boring. Father always loved the sports section, and Mother was interested in any news about food and cooking. David was now understanding how limited their realms were.

Cornelia surprised David with her answer: "I think the news is horrible. I would rather read or talk to my dolls and to Jessie. At least they respond when I talk to them. When Mom and Dad are watching the news they don't like it when anyone else says a word. And they don't even talk back to the news, they just sit there like zombies."

"That's an interesting description of them: Zombies! Why do you call them that?"

"Because they're alive but they act like they're dead. Zombies are the living dead. And when the news is on Mom and Dad are stuck to it like it was alive and they aren't. It's kind of scary actually."

"But don't they talk to each other about the news?" David asked.

"No, each one is interested in something different and they don't share their interests. They really act like they are dead to each other. I used to enjoy being with them, they were funny and talked to me a lot but then they got quieter and quieter and stopped reacting to things I would say. Why do people do that? Why do they become dead? Are only children really alive? And what happens to turn alive children into dead grownups?"

"Your questions and observations remind me that Grandfather knew what happened in our towns, and that was why he came for me. He knew that I wasn't completely dead yet but that I soon would be if I remained here any longer. Elephant knew that also, that is why he told me I would have to leave school and then I realized that I could not leave school without also leaving home. And the very next morning Grandfather was waiting for me saying that he had heard my call. But I hadn't called him. I didn't even know he existed. But somehow he must have known that I existed, and that my own aliveness would soon disappear unless something was done, so he came to rescue me."

"But how could he hear you from so far away?" Cornelia asked looking very puzzled.

"I don't understand it either," David replied. "He told me that everything is connected but that we have to be tuned in to the channel for knowing the connection. If we try to do everything only with our thinking then we lose the connection to that channel. He also told me that we think we are safe in our thinking and that we go there in order to feel safe, but that we are not really safe, in fact we are more vulnerable than ever, because we have given up one way of knowing for the sake of another, when we actually need everything we have in order to really know."

"So have Mom and Dad given up the way of knowing that keeps them connected, and so now they each live in their own disconnected worlds but they think they live with each other in the same world? Did they trade their connection for the safety of their own thinking? And why would they do that? And have they left their connection with us also? And is that what we're talking about right now? But why would a person do that? I feel my connection with you very loud and clear and that is why I was so very happy when you came back home. I knew I would be able to talk to you and that you would be able to hear me. And what is that connection that I feel with you, anyway?"

Feeling!

"Grandfather told me that there was an energy that connected everything in the world, actually, everything in the Universe. The Universe is the world of all the worlds together, and it also includes the space that holds them together."

"Grandfather said that what we think of as empty space is really the glue that hold everything together, including ourselves. And that this glue is an energy that is invisible to our eyes but not to or bodies. He said our bodies can see this energy and that is how he saw me even though I was really far away. He said my energy was really loud, in fact, my energy at that time was yelling, crying out to the rest of the Universe. And that is why he came to get me."

"Did he tell you how he had learned to see your energy? So how does your body see that energy? Are our bodies blind? Mom and Dad never told me about that energy. Is there an eye that we can open and close?"

"Grandfather told me that our blindness comes from the fact that we learn to think about that energy rather than to see it. He said our skin is like a giant eye that can see much more than we think. And that our thinking learns to doubt that that energy exists because it is invisible, and we have difficulty thinking about things that are invisible. Our thinking is used to connecting to things that we can see, or hear, or touch, but the energy that exists and that we become blind to is a feeling."

"He also said that as children we have feelings that grownups don't want to know about, feelings that make grownups uncomfortable because they have learned to hide, and to hide their ability to feel. He told me that the people I come from would rather be blind than to acknowledge that feelings are deeper than thinking. We have learned to think that thinking can do everything, but that is like a dog chasing its own tail. He said that when thinking learns to justify itself it then disconnects from our other ways of knowing."

"He told me that was why it was so important for me to take off my clothes when I went into the mountains or the sea, so that my entire body could remember to see again. He said clothes are like a blindfold that we put on our body, so no wonder we bump into the things that we forbid ourselves to see. He said the people that I come from try to hide the way a baby sees from the time it is born, but that they are really hiding their own blindness. He said our babies are deeply saddened by the way we treat them as if they were blind, as if their bodies can't see, and that we then treat the entire world that way. And that is how we lose our connection to everything. He said we are particularly brutal to those people that have retained their ability to see, and that in treating them as if they were blind we just show them our own arrogance and blindness."

More Feeling

"Wow! That's exciting! I think I've always known that my body can see but there seems to be no way to talk about that with Mom and Dad. I am so glad you've returned. There are so many things I need to hear from you. Grandfather sounds like a wonderful man. I do need to meet him! I do need to meet him!" Cornelia was beside herself with joy.

David heard Cornelia's words with a deeply satisfied understanding, and he realized there was hope for the world that he was born into. Not everyone ended up in the thinking prison as soon as they were born. He began to wonder if perhaps girls were more open to the way a body can see than boys were.

"Tell me what else Grandfather said about bodies being able to see!" Cornelia was ecstatic.

"Well, he said that there was one problem that came with this ability. And this happens primarily with people who have refused to recognize that the body can see."

"What is that?" asked Cornelia, deeply interested.

"Well, he said that the eye of the body can not only see, but that it can also send the energy that others see."

"But that sounds like a great gift! Then people can talk to each other invisibly, and over great distances. We wouldn't need telephones anymore!"

"The problem is that people don't learn the difference between the energy that they send and the energy that they receive. And that people who refuse to recognize that bodies can see also don't recognize the energies that they send."

"I don't really understand this," said Cornelia.

"Well, just because a person is blind to the energies doesn't mean that they stop sending or receiving those energies. But their thinking gets involved and thinks it can sort things out, but of course it can't. So thinking invents all kinds of stories to explain the things that happen as a result of this blindness."

"Grandfather said that thinking is like a sleep that people fall into, especially once their thinking is put down in signs and symbols. Then in that sleep they mistake their own thinking for the whole world, and they think that their thinking is more real than the world itself. He said that people in their blindness and sleep have killed each other without really understanding why they are doing so. And he said that the blindness of the body that children are first taught is the beginning of the sleep of thinking that they then fall into. He told me that his own people have suffered tremendously because of the storytelling sleep that the invaders brought with them."

Storytelling Sleep

"I don't really understand what you mean by 'storytelling sleep.'"

"What I mean, and what Grandfather understood, is that people get lost in the stories that they tell without realizing that it is just a story and not the world that all life except humans lives in. People tell stories, or hear stories, and then begin to believe that the stories are true. They begin to repeat the story to themselves and then act toward the world as if the story they are telling is more true than their own experience. And so people learn to carry around different stories, and when those stories don't agree with one another then people think that they themselves are in conflict. People get stuck in their own stories. This is the prison that Elephant and Grandfather helped me realize was being built around me in school. Grandfather helped me to understand that thinking is something organic, just like breathing is, and that school is used to train thinking as if it were a monkey in a circus, so that it will do its tricks.

Then it becomes automatic and mechanical, and the person thinks of themselves as educated, whereas they have actually sacrificed a great chunk of their own aliveness for the sake of this appearance. This is why Bearman and Grandfather went to such great lengths to help me realize that I needed to learn from myself, from my own experiences in nature, rather than thinking that someone else had all the answers and that to be educated was just a matter of repeating someone else's answers. To be intelligent really means that your own thinking is completely related to the rest of who you are, and that is different from being educated."

"That sounds complicated," said Cornelia sadly.

"It sounds that way when we focus on the words and the ideas rather than recognizing first of all what words and ideas are."

"What are they then?"

"Grandfather says that people are a unique kind of animal. We are an animal that talks. A lot. In fact most people have learned to talk continuously, silently, to themselves, and this is what we call thinking. He said that we first learned to talk in order to let people know what was going on with us inside. With our feelings and our experience and our awareness. And he said the ability to do this was really a great gift. But in talking we also need to learn to listen, and many people have learned to talk without listening."

"But people do listen," Cornelia blurted out.

"Yes, but many people only listen to their own talking. Or if they do listen, they listen through their own talking. They listen to hear if what someone else says is similar to or different from their own talking. So even though they seem to be listening they are only listening through the noise of their own talking and whatever they hear is relative to what they already think they know. So that people, little by little, get trapped in the stories that they tell over and over. And they feel comfortable in those stories only because the story is predictable. But it becomes predictable only because they tell it over and over, and this is how they form their own cages. They build their own cages and then think that they are safe in them."

"Oh, I see. They fall asleep inside of their own stories and this is storytelling sleep. I see now why Mom and dad are so boring. And why they like to watch the news so much. They look for things that fit in with the stories that they tell, and argue when the story is different. I often wondered why they get so angry sometimes at the man who is telling the news."

"Exactly! And in this way they have difficulty really

hearing me now, or you! They only want to hear the things that they already think. Anything else is unsafe."

"And this is why they have trouble listening to what Jessie tells me!" said Cornelia ecstatic.

"Yes, not only do they have trouble listening to other stories that don't fit in with their own, but their own stories include prohibitions against other things being able to talk. The stories they tell say that only they can think or talk. So this keeps them from really listening! And they call someone crazy who listens to the talking that everything in the world does. Everything talks in its own way, but people have invented a story that doesn't allow them to listen to anything other than people. So it's not that things can't talk, but that people have confused listening with talking, and their own listening has become deaf."

Deaf People and Written Stories

Cornelia was really excited. David had helped her understand why her mother and father seemed so dead. They weren't real zombies, she thought to herself, they had just learned to act like zombies, by limiting the things they could do or know. And they had done this by becoming deaf to the way everything in the world talks. And their deafness had been built by the stories they told about other things not being able to talk, when in fact it was they that had given up listening. They had given up listening to anything other than their own stories. Suddenly everything was beginning to make sense again. Cornelia was so grateful that David had returned. She realized he was teaching her things that no one else could. No one else except perhaps Grandfather.

"But how did you manage to stay out of this prison?" Cornelia asked.

"I always listened to Gordie and to Elephant, and I also talked to them and asked them questions," David replied.

"But why couldn't Mom and Dad do that too?"

"I think it was too late. In fact they began to look at me strangely whenever I told them what Gordie had said. So I stopped telling them about my talks with Gordie, and they never knew about Elephant. Somehow I knew if I told them they would get very upset. And I was right. I understand that now, but at that time it didn't make any sense to me. And it wasn't until I met Grandfather and Bearman that I understood that listening to the way everything talks is the way to stay connected to the world. Mother and Father used to call it making things up, but I see now that the stories they told themselves over and over was the real way of making things up. Listening to the world and hearing what it says is the way to stay connected. Unless you want to be a dog chasing its own tail."

David and Cornelia both laughed. But they also knew that what they were talking about was very serious.

And they were becoming more and more aware of the sad prisons that their mother and father lived in. And they also knew that mother and father would not feel safe until David and Cornelia told the same stories that they did. But

if they did then they would be sacrificing their own aliveness and intelligence.

Freedom from Thinking

"But you think very clearly. And it sounds like Grandfather also thought very clearly. How did your own thinking stay so free?"

"Grandfather told me that thinking is a great gift unless we get trapped in it. And the way not to get trapped is to stay out of it."

"But how can you stay out of it and still think?" Cornelia asked puzzled.

"Grandfather said by realizing that it is only one way of knowing, and not the deepest way," answered David.

"Are there other ways of knowing?"

"Yes, there are. We have many different parts of ourselves that are alive. And Grandfather taught me that to adhere to any single one of them, or even to only a few, makes us smaller than we really are. We should be so large that there is room in us for every different dimension of who we are, and we also need to know that we can travel freely to any part of ourselves that needs to be present in any given situation."

"How do we travel to any part of who we are?" Cornelia was more puzzled than ever now.

"That's the job of our awareness. Our awareness should be free enough and also slippery enough to be able to go wherever in us it is needed. The trouble with telling ourselves the same story over and over again is that our awareness itself gets frozen to only one aspect of who we are, and the rest of ourself then feels abandoned or ignored. And whatever any part of us feels, we feel. Grandfather said it is like being autistic. Autistic children perform the same act over and over again, he said, and we think there is something wrong with them; but we don't even notice ourselves telling the same story over and over. We don't even recognize our own autistic thinking. Thinking should be free, like water, and able to take on the form of whatever situation we want to think about. Or free to depict any situation we find ourselves in. He told me that very few people are at such a place because we live at a time when we confuse intelligence with various types of frozen thinking. And we have confused school with the ability to do repetitive thinking."

"He said the people I come from train their children from the time they are very young to repeat the same thing over and over again, and then are very proud when the child does so. This pride, Grandfather said, is very characteristic of people who are stuck inside themselves. They think that their own stuckness makes them better than others, and that people kill one another from that place of stuck pride. He said his people were forbidden to live their own lives because of where my people were stuck. And he said his own greatest sadness was for children who are deliberately frozen into only a small dimension of who they really are. He said a person who is whole, that is, all of whose living dimensions are fully in communication, can be completely trusted, because such a person is balanced and has a living center. But a person who is stuck in only a small part of who he is is always false, even to himself. And a person false to himself cannot be trusted."

Cornelia was overwhelmed to hear such a clear understanding of people. She was hearing things that she inherently knew but had never heard before. She felt like fresh clear water was washing through her entire being, and she was more determined now than ever to meet Grandfather. And she was so deeply happy that David had returned.

Bedtime

Bedtime arrived so swiftly that both David and Cornelia were surprised. The evening news had ended and Father and Mother had entered the kitchen and informed the children that it was bedtime.

After saying goodnight, Cornelia retired to her room, the room that had originally belonged to David. She was exhausted but at the same time felt elated, refreshed in a way that thrilled her. The future was exciting and enticing. She could hardly wait for tomorrow, and renewed talks about life and about people. Every cell in her body felt alive and vibrant. She had never felt so fresh before.

David went to bed again in the guest room, thrilled that he had such an intelligent sister. He felt that he and Cornelia met in a place that was clear and yet full of a vision of possibilities. He couldn't believe even now that such a young child could have such a deep understanding, but he did know that there was something frustrating about living with Mother and Father, something that cried out for clarity and communication, yet when this was attempted both of his parents seemed to close down in a frustrating and stuffy way. He realized that when with them there seemed to be no air to breathe, and it felt like trying to run through molasses. Cornelia had brought a refreshing new space into this home. He fell asleep easily and dreamed about the village.

Dream of the Village

David could see the village in the distance. He seemed to be flying high above it. Then he realized he was Eagle, surfing on the air. The air was a landscape he could feel, with various layers of density, and he instinctively moved his wings and feathers in order to maintain a position on the surface of the sea of air that supported him. He was amazed at the power of his wings; with a few beats he could climb from one level to another. But even more amazing was the precision of his vision. He could see the village in its entire breadth stretched out between the mountain and the sea, and at the same moment he could see very precisely what the various people below were doing. It was a kind of seeing that he had not known as a human.

He realized that the village seemed much older than he had remembered it. And suddenly he saw several large ships in the sea, ships with large sails. Many tiny humans were swarming into small rowboats that were traveling back and forth between the ships and the village. As he looked more closely he saw that many of the men were dressed as sailors and had beards. Many of them at the edge of the village carried rifles or swords. He didn't recognize anyone in the village and that surprised him because he had known everyone when he had lived there. A sudden realization jarred him: the village that he saw and the ships and all the people, were several hundred years before his time; he was looking into a scene from the past.

As he looked more precisely he saw that the sailors were not at all interested in the life of the village nor in the particular people that lived there, but they seemed glued to things in the village; they were going around touching some of the carved posts and handling various blankets, and even feeling some of the blankets and clothes and hats as the villagers were wearing them. This intrusiveness was exactly the opposite of the respect that he himself had known in the village. He realized what he was seeing was a meeting of two different kinds of people, of two different cultures, and that what each culture experienced was very different. The sailors had no sense of the depth of feeling in the village culture, and the village people did not initially realize that the sailors were hardened and coarse and saw the world only in terms of acquisition. He knew that the main perspective in the village was a deep respect for aliveness itself but the sailors seemed oblivious to the living people and only looked at things that were lifeless.

With his eagle eyes he saw that the sailors were arrogant and disrespectful toward the villagers, treating them like the goods they were inspecting, and that the villagers, with their natural respect for aliveness, were puzzle and perplexed. At one edge of the village David saw one of the sailors touching a young girl in an aggressive way and showing her his teeth. Her father standing nearby grabbed him and pulled him away. Surprised, the sailor pointed his weapon at the man and fired. Everyone in the village froze as he fell to the ground covered in blood. The two groups faced each other, the sailors with weapons drawn and the villagers not knowing how to respond. The tension seemed to cause the air itself to stand still, and Eagle sailed directly into the crowd. Eagle's claws raked across the face of the man who had fired opening deep cuts. The man dropped his weapon and grabbed at his face with both hands. Every eye was on Eagle and the sailors began a quick retreat to the boats that had carried them to the shore. The entire village knew that Nature had come to protect them and rushed at the sailors, pushing them toward the boats and sending them on their way.

David awoke, panting and sweating, he couldn't seem to breathe deep or fast enough. Opening his eyes he looked around the guest room, relieved to find himself here at his childhood home. But a part of him was still overlooking the village, aware of the conflict, and realizing that he was being called to action. He just didn't know what he was to do.

To be continued…

Something is Something is part two of a series of novels by Steve Gallegos that explores living with the Deep Imagination as a vital and alive part of human awareness.

Cornelia Meets Grandfather will be available by December 2014.

Resources

For information on Deep Imagery:

International Institute for Visualization Research
PO Box 632
Velarde NM 87582
www.deepimagery.org
www.facebook.com/deepimagery
IIVR@deepimagery.org

Eligio Stephen Gallegos, PhD,
PO Box 468
Velarde NM 87572
www.esgallegos.com
info@esgallegos.com

Books on Deep Imagery from Moon Bear Press:

Control and Obedience: The Human Illness
by E.S. Gallegos Ph.D. (2013)

Chakra Power Animals: The Living Energies of the Chakras
by E.S. Gallegos Ph.D. (in preparation)

The Personal Totempole Process: Animal Imagery, the Chakras and Psychotherapy
by E.S. Gallegos Ph.D. Kindle Edition (2013)

Animals of The Four Windows:
Integrating Thinking, Sensing, Feeling and Imagery
by E.S. Gallegos Ph.D. ISBN: 0944164404

Into Wholeness: The Path of Deep Imagery
by E.S. Gallegos Ph.D. ISBN 978-0944164228

Little Ed and Golden Bear
by E.S. Gallegos Ph.D. ISBN 978-0944164068

The Circus Cage: A Journey of Transformation
by Rosalie G. Douglas. ISBN 978-0944164020

Dancing in my Grandfather's Garden: Unearthing the Soul of the Feminine and the Gift of Deep Imagery,
by Phyllis Brooks Licis, ISBN 979-0944164181

Seeds of Enlightenment: Death, Rebirth, and Transformation through Imagery,
by Rene Pelleya-Kouri available on Kindle November 2013

www.ingramcontent.com/pod-product-compliance
Lightning Source LLC
Chambersburg PA
CBHW071358170626
46811CB00003B/1176